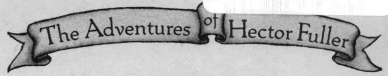

BOOK 1

Hector Springs Loose

The Adventures of Hector Fuller

BOOK 1

Hector Springs Loose

By Elizabeth Shreeve
Illustrated by Pamela Levy

To Phyllis Heidenreich Shreeve —E. S.

First Aladdin Paperbacks edition January 2004

Text copyright © 2004 by Elizabeth Shreeve
Illustrations copyright © 2004 by Pamela Levy

ALADDIN PAPERBACKS
An imprint of Simon & Schuster
Children's Publishing Division
1230 Avenue of the Americas
New York, NY 10020

Also available in an Aladdin Library edition
Designed by Debra Sfetsios
The text of this book was set in Graham.

Printed in the United States of America
2 4 6 8 10 9 7 5 3 1

The Library of Congress Control Number for the Library Edition is 2003106061
ISBN 0-689-86414-0

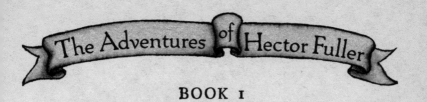

The Adventures of Hector Fuller

BOOK 1

Hector Springs Loose

Table of Contents

Chapter One

The Wumblebug Hole

Hector Fuller the wumblebug lived in a snug hole in the ground.

Like all bugs, Hector had six legs and a fine pair of antennae. Being a wumblebug—a home-loving creature you won't find in any book, except for this one of course—his front legs were useful for digging tunnels and caves. On his back were four small wings, so he could fly a little. But his belly was round and his legs a bit scrawny. In fact, he was no athlete and liked to stay close to the ground.

Hector's hole was well equipped and up-to-date. His tunnels let in plenty of fresh air, light, and delicious rainwater. He had a big, soft chair for reading and a small kitchen in which to make good things to eat. He was a happy

young bug, content in his hole, with a few friends and cousins nearby for company.

But there comes a day when adventure finds even the quietest home. A day that starts like any other but ends up in a totally new place.

That day came for Hector one morning in early spring.

Chapter Two

An Unwanted Guest

Hector sat at his piano, pounding out a noisy duet, with his four front feet on the keys and the bottom two on the pedals. A spring breeze drifted down his tunnel, making him restless for the first time in months.

Just as he reached the end of the song the piano began to rumble. The walls began to shake. The rumbling grew louder and louder, like thunder before a storm. Heavy footsteps galloped by overhead, followed by more trampling and the loud bark of a dog.

Ah, thought Hector. *The dog chasing deer from the garden.* The next moment the light from the tunnel went out. *Scritch-scritch-scratch-scritch* came a sound from above. The walls rattled some more.

"Just my luck," said Hector with a laugh. "He's sat down right on the tunnel. Now he's scratching . . . and soon I'll have light again." And sure enough, the dog gave one last growl, in case any deer were still listening, then trotted off. Light poured down the tunnel again.

With the light, however, came a small speck of dark. The speck dived down the tunnel and stopped to look around. Ignoring Hector, it pulled a tall hat down over its head, gathered its strong legs beneath it, and leaped clear across the room.

It was a hopping flea.

"Hello!" said Hector in surprise. "Can I help you with something?"

The hopping flea did not reply. He pulled a tiny tape measure from his pocket and sprang to the ceiling to measure the height. Then he darted across to the kitchen and over to a shelf of books.

"May I ask what you're doing?" said Hector. "Excuse me, but I don't think I invited you—"

The flea shot around the room again. Then he

leaped back to the tunnel and yelled in a high, squeaky voice, "Looks good, boys! Let 'er rip!"

"No!" cried Hector. "Stop!" He jumped down off the bench, ran to the tunnel, and looked up. Just in time for twelve more fleas and fifty-seven suitcases to tumble down on top of his head.

Chapter Three

A Terrible Itch

The fleas sprang to action at once.

Out of the suitcases came costumes, puppets, a small black cannon, and a big folding sign that said HOPPING FLEA CIRCUS: THE GREATEST LITTLE SHOW ON EARTH!

Within moments the room filled with fleas leaping in all directions with ropes, signs, banners, and poles. A unicyclist practiced riding upside down and backward over Hector's new carpet. A contortionist stretched herself into a hoop and rolled in wild circles around his reading chair.

"What are you doing?" cried Hector, almost speechless with shock. "You can't put up a circus here!"

"Heads up!" called the hopping flea, waving

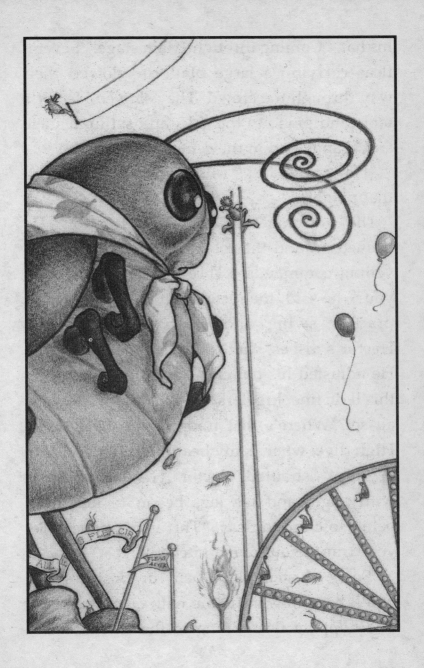

his hat. "Coming through! Main stage!" Several fleas carrying a large platform plowed their way through the crowd. They shoved Hector's table and piano to the side, and set up a stage and grandstand in the center of the room.

"Hey, watch out!" said Hector. "Don't touch that piano!"

The hopping flea paid no attention. He dashed around the room, directing traffic and yelling commands. "Throw me that line, will you?" he said, then leaped to the trapeze for a practice swing and crashed straight into Hector's dishes, neatly stacked above the sink. He adjusted his hat and stood up. "This'll do, this'll do fine. Jugglers, ready? Fire swallowers, all set? Where's that trampoline? Over there! High dive, where's my beautiful high dive?"

"Stop!" shouted Hector. His face flushed with anger and his legs began to itch from being so close to fleas. "This is my house! Get your trapeze out of my kitchen!"

"Sorry, mister. Not open for business yet. You'll have to wait in line with everyone else." The hopping flea sprang to the side as a flea clown on stilts came teetering through the crowd. "Okay, time for the cannon test! Where's that hoop? Got it burning? All right, ready for countdown! Four . . . three . . . two . . . one!"

The cannon exploded with a loud bang and a cloud of black smoke. A muscular flea flew through the air, missed the flaming hoop, and landed with a thud on a painting of Hector's grandmother.

"All right, boys, a little to the left next time!" called the hopping flea. "Okay, ladies and gents. Positions, please! It's show time!"

"Stupid fleas," muttered Hector, scratching his ankles. "Never listen. Now what am I going to do?"

"If I were you, buddy," said a low voice, "I'd make like a banana and split. Once the boss sets up, there's no stopping the Hopping Flea Circus."

Hector looked down. There, leaning against the wall, was a flea clown in face paint and a huge fake nose. He had two enormous shoes on his hind feet, and his front feet held a ukulele, a small guitar.

"What?" said Hector. "What do you mean?"

"I mean," said the clown, "that you may as well vacate the premises. Skedaddle! Find the door! Leave!" The clown began to strum the ukulele, playing a fast, twanging song that added to the noise. "A word to the wise, that's all. But it's your decision, wumblebug. Doesn't matter to me."

Hector looked around at the circus that had transformed his home. The opening act was up on the stage. Music was starting, and the first customers were filtering in. Hector tried waving to the bugs buying tickets from the hopping flea, but no one saw him and no one waved back.

"Can you believe it?" Hector said to the clown. "Too busy even to say hello. Some of my own friends, paying good money to watch a bunch of fleas wreck my place."

There was no answer. The clown was up on the main stage strumming the ukulele and turning somersaults in the opening parade.

Hector sighed and turned to his back tunnel, just missing a crash with an acrobat who had overshot the edge of the stage. He grabbed his backpack from its hook on the wall and threw in a pocketknife with scissors. Shoelaces. Crackers and gum. At the last moment he added a clump of dirt, a piece of the hole he had once called home.

Surely he could find another place somewhere out there in the world. A spring morning was the perfect time to try. With barely a glance Hector Fuller the wumblebug climbed from his flea-filled home and set off into the damp day.

Chapter Four

Slow Talker

Hector burst from his tunnel under a wide and windy sky. After the crowded hole a kind of buzzing energy filled his whole body. His legs itched and his antennae wiggled and his short wings unfolded in the morning sun, catching the breeze and lifting him into the air.

Rising unsteadily, Hector saw the garden, and beyond that a dark line of trees. He flapped his wings for a better view, then lurched sideways as his backpack swung him around. His head spun as he tumbled this way and that, carried by the wind.

Just below, a zigzag-striped snail slithered from under a wet leaf, leaving a trail of ooze that glistened in the morning light. The snail's eyeballs swiveled, one to the left and one to the

right, as he watched the wumblebug flutter and tip and tip and land on the ground with a bump. When he recognized Hector, both eyes poked up in surprise.

"Why . . . so . . . fast, . . . Hector?" he said with the terrible slowness of snails.

"I'm heading out," Hector answered, climbing to his feet and brushing himself off. "By foot, I think."

"You? But . . . why?"

"I need a new home, that's why." Hector's legs itched very much, and it was hard to stand there while the snail found his words.

"What's . . . wrong . . . with . . . the . . . old . . . one? . . . Seems . . . fine . . . to . . . me."

"That's what you think! It's not fine at all. A whole flea circus moved in. A circus—in my wumblebug hole! I'm surprised you're not there. Everyone else is, and they wouldn't even help me out."

The snail shook his head and neck. "Ohhhh . . . no. . . . A . . . circus . . . is . . . no . . . place . . . for . . . a . . . snail. . . . All . . . that . . . salt . . . on . . . the . . . popcorn. . . . Crowds . . ."

"Well, at least you still have a house. Some of us aren't so lucky. A wumblebug without a hole is like a . . . like a snail without a shell!"

"That . . . would . . . be . . . a . . . slug."

"Oh, you know what I mean!" grumbled Hector. He stamped his feet with impatience and scratched his ankles.

"Maybe . . . if . . . you . . . waited," said the snail, who did not seem to mind Hector's bad mood, "they'd . . . soon . . . be . . . gone. . . . You . . . could . . . stay . . . with . . . me. . . . We . . . could . . . talk. . . . You . . . know, . . . Hector, . . . it's . . . a . . . bug-eat-bug . . . world . . . out . . . there."

"I'm not worried. With a color like this, anyone would know I'm not good to eat." Hector waved at his back, which was bright red like a ladybug's. Then he stuck out his legs, which were swollen with little dots. "Now my legs are red too. See? Fleas make me itch, and if there's one thing I can't stand . . ."

"Aaahhhhh . . . ," said the snail, swiveling both his eyes in circles. "Allergic! . . . I've . . . got . . . just . . . the . . . thing."

"You do?" Hector leaned a little closer.

"Works . . . every . . . time. . . . Guaranteed. . . . What . . . you . . . need . . . for . . . that . . . rash . . . is . . . slime!" The snail began to produce a long tendril of ooze from under his shell.

"Oh, not slime!" Hector shuddered. "Thanks, but you know, I think I'll be okay."

"If . . . I . . . were . . . you, . . . Hector," said the snail, "I'd . . . go . . . back . . . and . . . see . . . if . . ."

The snail opened his mouth for some more slow words, but Hector was already gone. He didn't think about the snail's advice until much later. And then it made a lot more sense.

Chapter Five

Caterpillar

The first signs of spring greeted Hector all around. A few tender flowers reached up with trust to the sun. The low branches of blossoming plum trees gave a sweet smell to the air and sprinkled him with leftover raindrops as he trudged along.

At the edge of the garden Hector entered a small forest of grasses that rose straight up to the sky. From among the green growth came the sounds of the season—the building of nests and the chatter of new neighbors making plans for the months ahead.

Among these cheerful sounds Hector heard one faint, sad voice. He looked up. There was an orange-and-black-striped caterpillar swinging from a branch, moaning as if his heart would break.

"Good morning," said Hector, moving his head back and forth to follow the swaying form. "Something wrong?"

"Gone, all gone!" said the caterpillar.

"What's gone?"

"The last one! My family! Swallowed by sacks! Now I'm all alone." The caterpillar broke into sobs.

Hector reached into his pack for a cracker and held it out. "Here, try one. Tastes good when you're feeling sad."

"Good for what?"

"Why, to eat of course. For breakfast."

"Oh, heavens no, heavens no. Never touch the stuff. I am a caterpillar, you know. Or at least, I think I am. Oh, I'm so confused!" The caterpillar twisted upside down and began to cry again.

"I'm so sorry," said Hector. "Can I do anything to help?"

"There's nothing to do but wait." The caterpillar sniffed and rubbed his eyes. "Until I get swallowed up as well."

"Surely not! Isn't there something you can do?"

"Not a thing! Some of us make it, and some of us don't."

"Make what?"

"Butterflies. And then we fly away!"

"Butterflies?" said Hector. "That's not so bad!"

The caterpillar arched in the air toward Hector. His black eyes shone with tears. "How would you like to change that way?" he said in an angry voice. "Just when you'd gotten used to being a caterpillar. Gotten it all figured out. What to eat and so forth. Then all of a sudden, without anyone asking or giving you a choice, you get all wrapped up and can't talk to anyone, and . . . and . . . and . . . how will I even breathe? . . ." His voice broke off in a wail.

"Maybe it won't be so bad. Maybe . . . ," said Hector. But the caterpillar shook his head as he spoke, so that tears fell in a circle around the wumblebug's six feet. "Well, sure you don't want a cracker?"

"Heavens no, heavens no. I'm a bit tired,"

said the caterpillar, pulling himself up onto the branch. "But thanks, thanks, heavens yes, thanks." The caterpillar inched away. His dark bristles caught the light as he nibbled a leaf and slipped away into the shadows.

Chapter Six

The Tree

Hector stood still, staring at the branch where the caterpillar had swung a moment before. *Perhaps,* he thought, *a journey was not such a good idea.* He might get hungry and thirsty. Or lonely. Or cold. He might change, like the caterpillar. And it might even hurt.

On the other hand, if he turned back now, he could easily get home for lunch.

A small wind shook the branch and sent a shimmer of light onto Hector's feet. He looked down. There was the cracker, waiting to be eaten. There was the path ahead, ready for his step. And there—still itching and red—were his six strong legs.

There was no turning back. He must find a

new place, as far from the Hopping Flea Circus as he could possibly get.

Lunch would have to wait.

Hector pulled his pack more firmly onto his back and began to walk, letting thoughts come and go as they pleased. As the day wore on he began to think of home—the wumblebug hole he was leaving behind, safe and dry under the ground. His friends there—his favorite cousin, Suzy the ladybug, and his old friend Lance the lacewing. Could he ever find a place like that again? Where did he really belong?

As if in answer, Hector looked up. Before him, in the middle of a small clearing, stood a pine tree whose branches swept down to the ground. *Perhaps*, thought Hector, *perhaps a tree is the place for me. Perhaps I have spent too much time underground.*

The wumblebug set to climbing through the needles of the towering tree. Up and up he went until he grew dizzy and stopped to peek at the ground far below. At that moment a hummingbird zoomed past at top speed, her

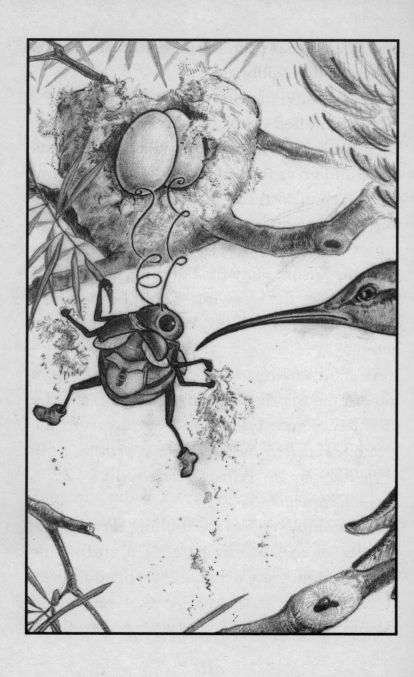

daggerlike beak outstretched. Hector ducked his head and cried out. He scrambled up the branch, slipping and grabbing on to sharp pine needles and the rough bark. Then he touched something else—something soft and light.

It was a tiny nest, hidden in a pocket of branches. And in the nest lay two pale blue eggs about the size of Hector himself.

"It's okay!" called Hector as the hummingbird darted and dipped and gathered speed for another attack. "I'm not after your eggs!"

The hummingbird dive-bombed again, this time so close that Hector slipped. As he fell, he grabbed and tore at the nest. The eggs tumbled and turned and came to rest on the very edge, held up by nothing but the tips of Hector's two antennae.

"My nest! My nest!" screamed the hummingbird in a high, piercing voice. Her spots of ruby red throat feathers flashed, and her words came so fast that Hector could barely understand. "My eggs! My eggs! Get away! Get away! Get away!"

"Wait! Slow down!" cried Hector, struggling to pull himself up without letting go of the eggs. "I'm so sorry! But please—let me get up!"

The furious bird raised her shoulders and thrust her sharp beak at Hector's belly, ready to spear him through.

Chapter Seven

Repair Work

The hummingbird hovered, unsure, her wings lost in a blur of speed. She always attacked anything that came close to her nest. But if Hector fell, so would the eggs.

While the bird decided, Hector pulled himself up. One leg, then another. One foot at a time. His heart pounded and his antennae shook, but he kept careful hold of the eggs.

Finally Hector got up over the edge. He stood in the nest, took a deep breath, and examined the damage. Not too bad—not for a wumblebug with a good set of tools.

"Look," he said to the hummingbird. She hovered close, staring at Hector with a mix of anger and uncertainty. "I can fix it. You see?"

Hector fumbled in his pack and pulled out his pocketknife with scissors.

"For free," he added in a small voice.

"Don't touch the eggs! Don't touch the eggs!" screamed the bird. Then in a flash she was gone.

Hector held his breath, waiting for a final attack. But when the hummingbird swooped back, her beak was full of moss and spiderweb and the soft, downy seeds of a thistle flower. "Do it now! Do it now!" she squeaked, dropping it all in a heap. "Don't touch the eggs! Don't touch the eggs! Don't touch the—"

"I won't," said Hector. "Now, the first thing is to—"

"Work fast! Work fast! Work—"

"Right, I hear you. Look, why don't you go get some . . . some more spiderweb?"

The hummingbird dashed off. Hector took a deep breath and began to lay out the pieces of moss and cut them to the right length. Then all too soon the bird was back, yelling in his ear again. "Here it is! Here it is! Fix it! Fix it! Fix it! Fix it!"

"Okay, okay," said Hector. "You know, I could work a lot better if you'd—"

"You broke it! You broke it! Hurry up! Hurry up! Hurry up!"

"Look," Hector said with a sigh. "How about some more . . . thistledown. Lots and lots, okay? Never can have too much thistledown, that's what I say."

The bird flew off again, leaving Hector alone with the quiet, sleeping eggs. The soft nest filled him with delight. Would not a tree house be the perfect home? Hector began to mend the tear in the nest, using spiderweb for thread. He trimmed the ends neatly with his scissors. Finally, he lined the inside with thistledown, wrapping it with more spiderweb to hold things securely in place.

When the hummingbird returned with her ninth or tenth load, the job was done and the tree was deep in shadows. Without a word of thanks, the bird turned her tail feathers to Hector and sat down on the nest.

"What do you think about a wumblebug for a neighbor?" asked Hector as he built a rough nest for himself. He had run out of spiderweb, but there was plenty of thistledown left. The hummingbird did not answer, so Hector went on. "See, I'm looking for a new home. My old place is a circus now. These fleas came and moved in like they owned it! Can you believe it?"

Again there was no reply. Peering through the growing darkness, he saw that the hummingbird was fast asleep.

Hector sighed and pulled a few crackers out of his pack for dinner. Then, feeling rather thirsty and alone, he settled in for the night.

Nothing is more important to a wumblebug than a good night's sleep in a warm and cozy place. High in the tree, Hector tossed from side to side as the evening breeze found its way through the branches. "Too much air all around," he muttered, pulling the thistledown closer and breaking it further to bits. The moss tickled his legs and started them itching again.

At last Hector fell into a broken sleep. Through the long night he waved his small wings as dreams sent him tumbling through the dagger-sharp needles of the tall pine tree.

Chapter Eight

Up, Up, and Away

Hector woke early, feeling thirsty but ready for whatever the day might bring. He rose and stretched, and looked out over the landscape around him. In the distance—impossibly far, it seemed—he spied a quiet pond. The sight made him thirstier still.

"Maybe," he said to no one but the eggs, "I can get to that pond and have a good drink. Maybe, if I hike all day."

Gathering up his pack, Hector started down the tree in short, fluttering jumps. He hadn't gone far before he saw a drop of dew hanging from the tip of a leaf. A fresh drink—right now!

Hector inched his way out and took a long, cool drink. Then, straightening up, he saw an even more wonderful sight.

In the warm spring sunshine a spider's nest stirred and opened. As Hector watched, out of the nest spilled hundreds of newborn spiderlings. They swarmed all over the branch, spinning their first lines of silk—the lines that take spiderlings out into the world, like tiny hot-air balloons.

The newborn spiders crawled over one another, crossing and tangling their lines. They argued with their brothers and sisters. And then, one by one, each spiderling climbed to a high spot and faced into the breeze. Away they soared, their long silk draglines waving in the morning air, keeping them afloat.

How beautiful! How brave! Hector tiptoed out closer. The leaf swayed beneath him, but all he noticed were the spiderlings, setting off to find their new lives. He leaned out as far as he could, waving with his four front feet. "Good luck!" he called. "Have a good flight!"

Suddenly the leaf snapped under Hector's feet, dropping him straight into the path of the flying spiderlings. A dragline caught his backpack and snatched him up into the air.

"Help!" cried Hector. "Help!"

"What are you doing?" yelled the spiderling to whom he was attached. "Get off!"

"I can't!" Hector reached for the dragline, but it tangled with his wings. "We're too high!"

"Use your wings!" The spiderling twisted and turned, searching for a stronger breeze to keep them aloft. Every move sent Hector swinging wildly through the air.

"I can't fly that far! My wings are tangled! Besides, I'm scared of heights!"

"Then, why were you up in that tree?"

"I was trying it out! I thought it might be a good home. But it wasn't—and this is much worse!" The tree now seemed like a safe and easy place compared with this terrible flight.

"You're pulling me down! Let go!" screamed the spiderling.

"I can't let go! I'll crash!" Hector hung on for dear life. He glanced down at the ground far below and gulped with fear. When he looked up, he saw the dragline growing thinner as it pulled and stretched with his weight. "Please— don't let me fall!"

"Can't help it! We're out of control!"

Down they looped, lower and lower, heading for a crash. At last the dragline reached its limit and broke. They parted. The spiderling lifted up into the sky. Hector fell free into the vast, empty space below.

Chapter Nine

Splashdown

Down Hector fell, past birds and the tops of trees. Down he fell, struggling to free his wings from the broken dragline. The land zoomed closer. He fought and fluttered as best he could. Finally he took one last look at the blue sky and shut his eyes.

Splash! Hector landed in water. He sank. Still farther he fell, now into the dark, cold water of a pond. He touched bottom and rose, sputtering and gasping for air. He struggled to swim and sank again, past tadpoles and water plants waving from the bottom like flags. Coming up, he paddled furiously to catch a ripple, a small wave headed for shore.

By the time Hector pulled himself onto the shore, he was shaky with hunger and fright. He threw himself on a small patch of sand and

checked each leg. All there. Antennae and wings. Backpack. All there.

He was all in one piece and alive. In fact, he was sitting at the edge of the very same pond he had seen that morning from the branches of the tall pine tree.

Hector pulled open his wet pack and found his few remaining crackers. They were soggy, but he gobbled them down and took a sip of water from the pond. Feeling much better, he leaned against a blade of grass and soaked in the sun. He picked up a few rocks from the shore and tossed them into the water.

Plip! Plop! Ploop! The rocks made different sounds, depending on their size and shape. He tossed a few more. *Blurp! Plunk! Ping!*

Next he skipped some flat ones over the surface, making rippling puddles, five or six in a row.

Suddenly, up from the puddles popped the dark heads and shoulders of two water boatmen—slender beetles built for speeding across the water. Each spit out one of Hector's rocks.

Each rock hit the other one smack in the face.

"Oops," said Hector. "That was a big mistake."

Chapter Ten

Water Sports

The water boatmen glared at each other and raised their fists for a fight.

"Why did you do that?" said one to the other.

"Do what?" the other replied.

"Hit me with a rock, that's what!"

"I didn't. You hit me!"

"No, you hit me!"

"Did not!"

"Did!"

"Wait!" called Hector from the water's edge. "It was me, throwing rocks. Sorry! I didn't know you were there."

The water boatmen paddled over to Hector, using their long back legs like oars. They both had sporty racing stripes down their backs. One had a green stripe and the other had brown.

"That was you, was it? Don't throw stones in the training area!" said Brown Stripe.

"He wasn't throwing stones," said Green Stripe. "Only pebbles!"

"They were bigger than pebbles. They were stones!"

"Pebbles!"

"Stones!"

"It doesn't matter," said Hector. "I won't do it again. Can you tell me something about this pond? What's the neighborhood like? How do you spend your time?"

"Let me tell you . . . ," said Green Stripe, paddling in small circles.

"No, I'll tell him." Brown Stripe circled in the opposite direction.

"Why you?"

"I won the last race."

"You did not!"

"I did!"

"Oh, please," interrupted Hector. "I don't care about that. Tell me, what is there to eat? Can you show me?"

"I'll go!" they both yelled, and darted straight

to the bottom. Hector could see them there, grabbing up water plants. They popped their heads up again.

"We eat this." Brown Stripe handed Hector some slimy green algae dripping with mud.

"But we like this better." Green Stripe held up another plant that looked just as bad. "For the athlete in training this one's better. More vitamins."

"And who won the sprints last week? Hmm?" Brown Stripe glared at his racing partner.

"And who won for three weeks before that? Hmmmm?" Green Stripe glared back.

"I'd love to see you," said Hector. "Race, that is."

Without another word the water boatmen paddled out from shore and lined up.

"We're waiting!" they called.

"For what?" Hector called back.

"For you to start the race!"

"Oh! All right. Ready, set, go!"

The water boatmen shot down the pond, leaving two smooth silver lines in their wake. One pulled ahead, then the other. They disappeared down the long stretch of water, curved around, and sped back to Hector, waiting on the shore.

"Where's . . . the . . . finish . . . line?" they panted.

"How about right here?" Hector raised a stick in the air. "I declare . . . a tie!"

"A tie?" said Brown Stripe. "I finished first!"

"You heard the wumblebug," said Green Stripe. "It was a tie!"

"Was not!"

"Was too!"

"Liar!"

"Cheater!"

"It doesn't matter!" said Hector. "You both won. That was great! Tell me—how do you stay afloat? When I'm in the water, I sink."

"Air bubbles of course. See?" Green Stripe pulled alongside Hector and lifted his wings. "That's all it takes! Two or three should do it."

"No, no," said Brown Stripe. "He's bigger than we are. He'll need at least four!"

"You're crazy!"

"You're wrong. Here, try this." Brown Stripe scooped up some air bubbles and held them out. Hector tiptoed into the water. He raised his wings, tucked the bubbles underneath, and pushed off with his feet. Immediately he tipped head over heels. And there he stayed, trapped, his face down in the pond and his rear legs kicking wildly in the air.

The water boatmen pulled Hector right side up. They were both laughing hard.

"What's so funny?" said Hector, still sputtering.

"I love when that happens!" said Brown Stripe. "Always does with bugs shaped like you."

"Not always," said Green Stripe.

"Always."

"No. Remember that time when—"

"Oh, stop arguing!" grumbled Hector. "Why don't you go race each other in circles. All the way around the pond. Five times. Ten. And don't come back. Ready, set, go!"

The water boatmen raced off, leaving two silver streaks and the echo of their argument behind.

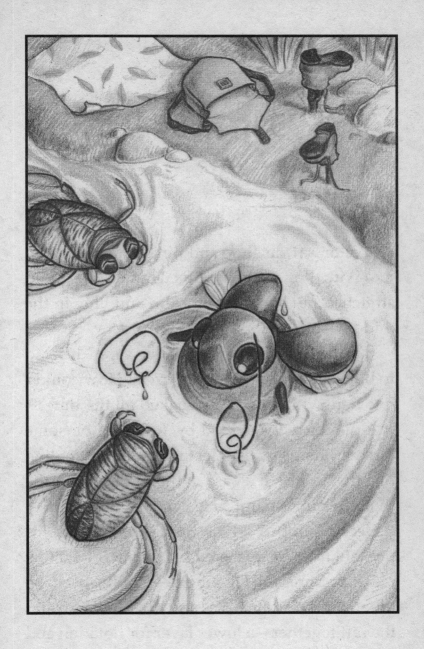

Chapter Eleven

The Pond

Hector sat on the sand, enjoying the quiet. With the water boatmen gone, the pond stretched out smooth and calm and blue in the midday sun.

"I'm not a swimmer, that's for sure," he said to himself. "But this pond is great. How could I live here without getting soaked all the time?"

A pile of twigs drifted by, followed by some broken bits of reeds. Hector imagined floating like that, without a care in the world. Then the thought came—a raft! He could build a raft!

Hector jumped to his feet. Pulling out his pocket-knife, he gathered a big pile of hollow reeds and grasses. Digging deep in his pack, he found the extra shoelaces and used them to bind the raft together—a lower layer for flotation and a dry surface on which to live. P[...] pulling, antennae waving, Hector la[...] new raft, jumped aboard, and wobble[...] the pond.

Life on the water seemed fine. Up ahead a mother duck led her fluffy ducklings across the pond. The young ones followed, pushing and bumping one another to find a better place in line. Hector dipped in a few of his feet. Then, gaining strength, he paddled hard out toward the middle.

At the sight of Hector, the mother duck arched her neck and spoke. "And who might *you* be, wumblebug?"

"Excuse me," said Hector, scrambling to his feet. "I'm Hector. I'm hoping . . . I mean, would this pond be a place for me? I'm looking for a new home."

"You'll have to ask the bullfrog," said the duck, shaking her head a little. "He's the senior."

"The senior?" Hector remembered something about the enormous appetites of frogs. "Please, could you tell me where he might be?"

"He'll be under the willow tree, of course," she snapped, as if Hector should already know.

"Thank you, I'm . . . ," Hector said, but the duck family had already glided away.

Hector aimed his raft toward a huge tree on the opposite shore. He paddled slowly. Dragonflies hovered and swooped. Light flickered on the water. Hector stretched out and watched clouds float by, dreaming of a new life on the pond.

Chapter Twelve

Senior Bullfrog

"RIBBIT!"

Hector jumped straight in the air.

The raft had run aground directly under the willow. Ahead sat an enormous green bullfrog surrounded by the cast-off legs of a dozen water striders that he had eaten for lunch.

Hector shuddered, cleared his throat, and gathered his courage to speak. "Good afternoon . . . good evening . . . umm, hello." No answer came from the frog, who frowned and stared as if trying to figure out what sort of bug Hector might be. And whether he might taste good.

"Umm, excuse me, sir," said Hector. "I'd like to use this pond, this one we're on, I mean, for my raft. As a place to live."

The bullfrog's eyes flickered. Quick as a flash

his great, sticky tongue shot out, grabbed a water strider skating across the pond's surface, and slurped it back into his mouth.

"Oh!" said Hector, pitching sideways on his raft. "You're hungry? Somewhere in here . . ." He dug in his pack as the unfortunate water strider slid down the bullfrog's throat. "Here we are. Would you like some gum?"

Hector tossed a piece, nearly losing his balance and falling into the water. The bullfrog's frowning mouth opened and his tongue flew out again.

"Do you like it?" asked Hector after the frog had chewed and chewed and chewed some more.

The bullfrog's frown grew deeper. He stared at Hector's bag. Finally he spoke with a booming voice. "Pig squash."

"What's that? Excuse me?"

"Pig squash," burped the great voice. "Want more, wumblebug."

"More? What? Oh, the gum?" Hector's voice squeaked.

"More wumblebug!" For a moment the bull-

frog fixed his bulging eyes directly on Hector.

A moment was more than enough. Hurling his last piece of gum at the frowning amphibian, Hector grabbed his pack, pushed off from his raft, and flew for the far shore as he had never flown before.

Chapter Thirteen

Homesick

Hector barely made it. Halfway across the pond his small wings began to ache and slow. All around him was water. Not far away was a bullfrog with a bottomless appetite and a lightning tongue.

But there, coming close, was the duck family out for an evening swim. Just as Hector's wings refused to flap one more time the ducks passed below. He plopped onto the smooth brown feathers of the mother duck and settled down with a deep sigh of relief.

Like the experienced mother she was, the duck ruffled her feathers, shook her head, and continued on a perfect glide. As they neared the shore Hector mumbled, "Thanks," and jumped to the bank. He lay there shivering, letting the last of the day's sun warm his aching wings.

Hector spent a soggy, miserable night huddled at the water's edge. He woke to a chilly fog. For the first time a tremendous homesickness came over him. He missed his hole. He missed his friends and the good feeling that a wumblebug gets from digging a tunnel. What was worse, he had run out of crackers and he had no idea how to get home.

Slumped over his pack, Hector's eyes fell on the clump of dirt from his hole. Thrusting his whole face and antennae into the pack, Hector inhaled the smell of caves, tunnels, and earth. He pulled out the clump and took a long, deep breath.

Perhaps it was the damp air—or maybe his hunger—that sharpened his senses. Suddenly, with all his heart, Hector knew he could get home. And that was where he wanted to be. Better to stand up to fleas than wander the wide world alone. Better to start digging all over again in a place he liked. With friends he loved. Better to make the long journey home than . . .

"Hello there!" came a voice. Hector stood up. There were the water boatmen, splashing their way across the foggy surface of the pond.

"Come on out!" called one. "The water's perfect. Flat and calm!"

"Not very calm, but flat!" called the other.

"Don't be ridiculous, it can't be calm unless it's flat!" said the first one.

"Can!"

"Can't!"

Hector shook his head. "No, no. Not for me," he said, as the water boatmen glided up to the shore. "I'm no water bug. Not a tree bug either, come to think of it. I'm a wumblebug, and I'm going home."

Hector pulled on his empty pack and turned back to the road.

Chapter Fourteen

Follow Your Nose

All day and all night Hector walked, his nose and antennae straight ahead. One foot, then another, and another and another and another and another. Somehow he knew that if he stopped, he might never make it home again.

On he walked, past the young spider's first tiny web, hanging with water drops that caught the morning light.

On past the tall pine tree, where the hummingbird swooped low and threw a heap of thistledown on his head. Without missing a step, Hector stuffed the soft stuff into his pack and added the ruby red feather that drifted along as well.

On into the night he walked, slower and

slower, as if in a dream. He was tired and sore. He began to smell familiar places, and it made him want to rest.

Perhaps, he thought in the darkest hour, *if I lie down here, they'll find me. It's not so far, after all. Perhaps . . .*

Hector's eyes closed, and sleep reached out for him, even as he walked. At that moment a butterfly circled overhead. The butterfly saw Hector stumble and slump toward the ground. He came closer and flapped his orange wings in the wumblebug's face, flickering him awake.

Hector kept going into the rising dawn. At last he drew near to the garden and then to the mouth of his very own hole. Staggering by now, he saw a small, sad group of bugs. At their center was a plump and lovely ladybug, wiping her tears with a clover leaf.

"Suzy! Lance!" cried Hector. His legs gave way and he fell into a heap on the ground.

His friends rushed to his side. "Hector! Hector! You're home!"

"Are they still here?" whispered Hector.

"Who, Hector?" said Suzy, holding on to

Hector as if she would never let go.

"The fleas. The Hopping Flea Circus that took my home."

"Oh, Hector, you silly bug," said Suzy. "All you needed to do was wait. You know fleas— here today, gone tomorrow. They've probably opened their circus five or six times by now. Down the road. Someplace else."

"They were fun, though," said Lance. "And the cotton candy was great."

"They're gone?" asked Hector.

"Long gone," said Lance.

"Of course," said Suzy. "We've scrubbed and we've cleaned, and everything is better than new."

With this good news Hector fell into a faint.

Chapter Fifteen

Home Cooking

Hector Fuller the wumblebug opened his eyes many hours later, not knowing quite where he was. Evening light slanted across the room. In his big chair sat Suzy, reading a book. In the kitchen was Lance, banging pots and spoons. Hearing Hector stir, his friends looked up and waited for him to speak.

"Hi," said Hector, his voice cracking. "Did I sleep all day?"

"All day, all night, and then all day again. Are you all right?" asked Suzy. "Does anything hurt?"

"I'm okay." Hector sat up. For a moment he saw his old home with new eyes—his piano bench with its soft cushion, a bowl on the table filled with a single ripe strawberry, the new tunnel he had just started to dig. Tears filled his eyes.

"I'm just glad to be here. I had lots of adventures. Look," he said, pulling the thistledown out of his pack. "Look at this stuff. Feel how soft! You weave it together with spiderweb. From now on we'll have the very best pillows and beds."

"Where did you find it?" Suzy squished thistledown between her front legs. "It's wonderful! Try it, Lance!"

"A hummingbird taught me," said Hector. "Not a friendly bird, but she had excellent ideas for nests. Next time maybe you'll come and I'll show you—the tree, the pond. Water boatmen who race on the water, and a duck . . . and . . . and we'll go together!"

"You must have traveled a long way, Hector. Sounds dangerous to me."

"Oh, not so bad," said Hector. "Not dangerous, as long as you know the way home."

His friends smiled and their antennae lifted. "Sounds good," said Lance. "To take a trip like

that. In the meantime—you hungry?"

Hector relaxed in the warm glow and inhaled the delicious smell of Lance's cooking.

"Starving," he said. "Let's eat."

Elizabeth Shreeve grew up in a family of writers and scientists who taught her to chase butterflies and otherwise scare the daylights out of small creatures in the local marshes and fields. She also liked to read and would have become a librarian if books could be stored outdoors. A graduate of Harvard College and the Harvard Graduate School of Design, she balances a career in environmental design with writing stories and reading in silly voices to her husband and sons. The origin of Hector Fuller's name and species is a closely-held family secret that Elizabeth is happy to share at book signings and school visits, where she talks with children about the natural world, the life of a writer, and the joys of becoming a life-long reader.

A r e   Y o u

Ready-for-Chapters

Page-turning step-up books for kids ready to tackle something more challenging than beginning readers

The Cobble Street Cousins
by Cynthia Rylant
illustrated by
Wendy Anderson Halperin
#1 In Aunt Lucy's Kitchen
0-689-81708-8

#2 A Little Shopping
0-689-81709-6

#3 Special Gifts
0-689-81715-0

The Werewolf Club
by Daniel Pinkwater
illustrated by Jill Pinkwater
#1 The Magic Pretzel
0-689-83790-9

#2 The Lunchroom of Doom
0-689-83845-X

Third-Grade Detectives
by George Edward Stanley
illustrated by
Salvatore Murdocca
#1 The Clue of the Left-Handed Envelope
0-689-82194-8

#2 The Puzzle of the Pretty Pink Handkerchief
0-689-82232-4

Annabel the Actress:
Starring in Gorilla My Dreams
by Ellen Conford
illustrated by
Renee W. Andriani
0-689-83883-2

The Courage of Sarah Noble
by Alice Dalgliesh
0-689-71540-4

The Bears on Hemlock Mountain
by Alice Dalgliesh
0-689-71604-4

Ready-for-Chapters

ALADDIN PAPERBACKS
Simon & Schuster Children's Publishing • www.SimonSaysKids.com

Read Aladdin Paperbacks' classic biography series,

Childhood of Famous Americans

See your local
bookseller for a full list
of available titles.

Aladdin Paperbacks
Simon & Schuster Children's Publishing
www.SimonSaysKids.com